THE MAGIC PAINTBRUSH

A CHINESE FOLKTALE

Retold by M. J. York • Illustrated by Cat Zaza

The Child's World®
1980 Lookout Drive • Mankato, MN 56003-1705
800-599-READ • www.childsworld.com

Acknowledgments
The Child's World®: Mary Berendes, Publishing Director
The Design Lab: Kathleen Petelinsek, Design
Red Line Editorial: Editorial direction

ISBN 9781614732204
LCCN 2012932438

Printed in the United States of America
Mankato, MN
July 2012
PA02123

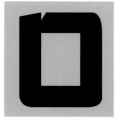nce upon a time, a boy named Ma Ling lived in China. Ma Ling was an orphan. He was poor, but he was polite and he was kind and he wished to help other people. He had no one to take care of him. He gathered firewood and herded cattle to earn his keep.

More than anything else, Ma Ling wished to become a painter. But his clothes were shabby and he had no money. No painter would teach him. And he did not have enough money to buy paints or a paintbrush.

Ma Ling asked the village schoolmaster if he could have a small, old brush. But the schoolmaster refused. "What could an orphan boy like you know about painting?" he sneered. But Ma Ling was still determined to be a painter.

So he scratched pictures of mountains and oceans in the mud. He took branches after they burned in a fire and used the black ends to draw birds and deer. He even wet his finger and used the water to draw flowers and fish on rocks.

One night, after a long day of working and drawing, Ma Ling fell into a deep sleep. He dreamed he was visited by a kind old man. In the dream, the old man handed Ma Ling a paintbrush.

"This paintbrush can do much good," whispered the old man, and the dream faded away. When Ma Ling awoke, he was grasping a paintbrush. It was small and old, and it was missing half its bristles. But it was a paintbrush, and it made Ma Ling very happy.

Ma Ling took ashes and water and
made ink. He dipped the brush and then
began to paint on a flat, white rock. His
brushstrokes quickly outlined a bird.
When he completed the final feather, the
bird chirped and flew away!

Ma Ling could hardly believe it. He thought he must be dreaming, so he decided to test the brush again. Once again, he dipped his brush in the ink. Once again, he began to paint on the flat, white rock. His brushstrokes quickly outlined a deer. When he added the last spot, the deer sprang from the rock and leapt away.

"It is a magic paintbrush!" exclaimed Ma Ling. He went to the village and began to help people. When he saw a child, he painted a toy. When he saw a hungry person, he painted rice and tea. And when he saw a farmer, he painted cows and new iron plows. With help from Ma Ling and his magic paintbrush, the people of the village began to prosper.

Before long, word of Ma Ling and his magic paintbrush reached the emperor. The emperor was a greedy man. He wanted all the riches and all the magic in the world for himself. He wanted Ma Ling's magic paintbrush badly.

Soldiers came to Ma Ling's village and grabbed Ma Ling. Ma Ling held tight to his paintbrush. The soldiers took the boy to the emperor's palace.

When they arrived, Ma Ling bowed to the emperor. "How can I be of service, Oh wise emperor?" he asked.

"Paint me a dragon!" ordered the emperor.

Ma Ling realized the emperor was cruel and greedy. Instead of a dragon, he painted a spiny lizard. The lizard flicked its tongue and sauntered off.

The emperor was furious that Ma Ling had disobeyed him. He took the magic paintbrush. He had Ma Ling thrown in a dungeon. Then, the emperor gave the magic paintbrush to a famous artist. The emperor ordered the artist to paint him piles of gold coins. The artist obeyed, but every coin he painted turned into an ordinary rock.

The emperor realized the paintbrush only worked for Ma Ling. Soldiers brought Ma Ling to the emperor again. The emperor said, "Ma Ling, if you paint what I ask I will send you home to your village."

Ma Ling knew the emperor would never let him go home as long as he had the magic paintbrush. He pretended to agree with the emperor.

The emperor made his first request. "Paint me a tree made of silver and a mountain made of gold," he ordered. The soldiers brought soft, white paper and fine colored inks. Ma Ling began his task, and the emperor looked over his shoulder.

First, Ma Ling painted a wide ocean. The emperor exclaimed, "Where is my tree?"

"Have patience," Ma Ling replied. Then, he painted an island in the ocean. On the island were trees made of silver and mountains made of gold.

"That's better," said the emperor. "Now paint me a boat so I can cross the ocean!"

So Ma Ling painted a fine sailboat. It had large red sails and a dragon's head on its prow. The emperor approved of Ma Ling's work. He boarded the boat.

"Now, send me a breeze to blow me to the island," he demanded.

So Ma Ling added wispy, curved lines, and the boat slowly moved away from shore.

"Faster, faster!" cried the emperor, impatient with greed.

So Ma Ling drew more lines and made them longer and bolder than the first lines. The wind blew harder, and the boat moved more quickly toward the island.

But the emperor still called for more wind.

Ma Ling added more and more lines until the wind blew with the strength of ten hurricanes. The ship sped toward the island over the choppy sea. But then, the strongest gust of all caught the ship's sail. The ship flipped over and sank. The emperor swam ashore on the island, alone with his trees of silver and his mountains of gold.

And Ma Ling traveled from village to village, painting toys for the children, tea and rice for the hungry, and beautiful birds and flowers for everyone's delight.

China

FOLKTALES

Do you like to draw or paint? In *The Magic Paintbrush*, the main character, Ma Ling, is very creative since he has no money to buy a paintbrush or pencils for drawing. He uses twigs, his wet finger, and even burned wood to make pictures. What other found items could you draw with?

The Magic Paintbrush is a folktale that originated in China, a country located in East Asia that has the largest population (or number of people who live there) in the world. *The Magic Paintbrush* became so popular through years of telling that the story is still told today. Folktales often have heroes, like Ma Ling, and they stretch our imaginations through fantasy. Things that can't happen in real life happen to characters in folktales: little boys fly, animals talk, and, as in this story, paintbrushes are magical. Folktales also teach us lessons about being kind and generous. They are fun to read so we remember these good lessons.

When the old man in Ma Ling's dream gives him a magic paintbrush that brings things to life, Ma Ling uses it for good. He paints toys for children and food for the hungry. But when a greedy emperor demands selfish things, he tricks him into becoming stranded on a deserted island. Ma Ling then is free to use his paintbrush wherever he wants, and continues to help the poor in many villages throughout China.

If you had a magic paintbrush, what would you paint?

ABOUT THE ILLUSTRATOR

Cat Zaza is an Italian illustrator, but she spent most of her life living all around the world. She currently lives in Paris, though she travels constantly. Cat enjoys learning everything she can about different cultures, and, true to her name, she loves cats!